In a Minute

illustrated by
Shelagh McNicholas

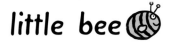

At 7:32 (and 15 seconds), Mum put her head round the door and shouted, "Molly! Time for bed! "Wash your face, brush your teeth...

make sure the bath is empty, pick up ALL your clothes...

and your books...

...tidy away your toys, give Dolly a kiss, **and get into bed!**

"I'll be up to read you a story!"

"In a minute!!!" She hollered.

Molly was very busy.
(Molly was always busy)

"A minute," thought Molly.

"Time to make myself look nice."

Molly thought that she
might use lipstick, mascara,
cotton wool, two boxes of tissues,
and a bottle of perfume.

Lovely black eyeliner (just like Mummy)

Beautiful lips (and a kiss for Mummy)

Perfect!

"A minute," thought Molly.
"Time to clean the bathroom."

Molly thought that she
ought to clean the bath, the sink,
the walls, two bars of soap,
and her favourite bear.

Scrub the taps (and shampoo the carpet.)

Polish the walls (and dry the carpet.)

That'll do...

"A minute," thought Molly.
"Time to do some washing."

Molly thought that she
should wash her shirts,
socks, jumpers, two
colouring in books, and her trainers.

Into the machine (turn ALL the dials.)

Add the powder (empty the box.)

Done...

"A minute," thought Molly.
"Time to bake something nice."

Molly thought that she would
need flour, jam, eggs, two slices
of bread, and a packet of crisps.

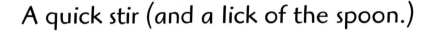

A quick stir (and a lick of the spoon.)

Into the dish
(just time to lick the bowl.)

At 7:48 (and 21 seconds)
Mum put her head round
the door and shouted,

"Molly...?!"

At 7:51 (and 49 seconds),
Mum put her head
round Molly's door.

"Good night, sleep well Molly,"
said Mum and she kissed her gently.

But Molly was fast asleep...

(since exactly one minute ago.)

For Maisie and Tom

First published in 2004 by Meadowside Children's Books
185 Fleet Street,London EC4A 2HS
This edition published in 2006 by Little Bee,
an imprint of Meadowside Children's Books

Text © Beth Shoshan 2004
Illustrations © Shelagh McNicholas 2004

The rights of Beth Shoshan and Shelagh McNicholas to be identified as the author
and illustrator of this work have been asserted by them in accordance
with the Copyright, Designs and Patents Act, 1988

A CIP catalogue record for this book
is availablefrom the British Library
Printed in China

10 9 8 7 6 5 4 3 2